ABOUT THE BANK STREET READY-TO-READ SERIES

More than seventy-five years of educational research, innovative teaching, and quality publishing have earned The Bank Street College of Education its reputation as America's most trusted name in early childhood education.

Because no two children are exactly alike in their development, the Bank Street Ready-to-Read series is written on three levels to accommodate the individual stages of reading readiness of children ages three through eight.

● *Level 1:* GETTING READY TO READ (Pre-K–Grade 1)
Level 1 books are perfect for reading aloud with children who are getting ready to read or just starting to read words or phrases. These books feature large type, repetition, and simple sentences.

● *Level 2:* READING TOGETHER (Grades 1–3)
These books have slightly smaller type and longer sentences. They are ideal for children beginning to read by themselves who may need help.

○ *Level 3:* I CAN READ IT MYSELF (Grades 2–3)
These stories are just right for children who can read independently. They offer more complex and challenging stories and sentences.

All three levels of The Bank Street Ready-to-Read books make it easy to select the books most appropriate for your child's development and enable him or her to grow with the series step by step. The levels purposely overlap to reinforce skills and further encourage reading.

We feel that making reading fun is the single most important thing anyone can do to help children become good readers. We hope you will become part of Bank Street's long tradition of learning through sharing.

The Bank Street College of Education

For my awesome Altmen,
with Love
—E.S.

REAL LIVE MONSTERS!

A Bantam Book/September 1995

Published by Bantam Doubleday Dell Books
for Young Readers, a division of Bantam
Doubleday Dell Publishing Group, Inc.
1540 Broadway, New York, New York 10036.

Special thanks to Hope Innelli
and Kathy Huck.

Library of Congress Cataloging-in-Publication Data

Schecter, Ellen.
Real live monsters! / by Ellen Schecter ;
illustrated by Donna Braginetz.
p.   cm.—(Bank Street ready-to-read)
"A Byron Preiss Book."
ISBN 0-553-09742-3 (hard cover).—
ISBN 0-553-37574-1 (trade paper)
1. Animals—Miscellanea—Juvenile literature.
[1. Animals—Miscellanea.]   I. Braginetz, Donna, ill.
II. Title.   III. Series.
QL49.S26   1995
591—dc20
94-23276   CIP   AC

Published simultaneously in the United States and Canada

PRINTED IN THE UNITED STATES OF AMERICA

0 9 8 7 6 5 4 3 2 1

Bank Street Ready-to-Read™

REAL LIVE MONSTERS!

by Ellen Schecter
Illustrated by Donna Braginetz

A Byron Preiss Book

BANTAM BOOKS
NEW YORK • TORONTO • LONDON • SYDNEY • AUCKLAND

CONTENTS

INTRODUCTION: MEET SOME REAL LIVE MONSTERS!

This book is about monsters:
creatures that look
SCARY, WEIRD, or *wild*.
But they are ***not*** creatures
out of nightmares.
They are alive somewhere
in the world . . . **right now . . . today!**

These real live monsters may make your hair
STAND ON END.
But when you know more about them,
you may change your mind.
You may think they're
AWESOME instead of AWFUL.

Read on . . . then decide for yourself!

CHAPTER ONE:
MIGHTY MINI-MONSTERS!

GIANT ATLAS MOTH
(Atlas attacus)
Southeast Asia

Is it a bird?
A toy plane?
Maybe a kite?
No, it's a moth!

Because of its 10-inch wingspan, you
could mistake an Atlas moth for a bird.
Its wing tips look like snake heads,
which helps scare enemies away.
Its brownish colors help it
hide on dry leaves under trees.

Like all moths and butterflies,
the Atlas moth has clear, thin wings
covered with colored scales.
A "window" in each wing lets
leaves on the ground show through.

Can you find a life-size Atlas moth
hiding in this picture?

What do you think:
AWFUL . . . or *awesome?*

GOLIATH BEETLE
(Goliathus giganteus)
Equatorial Africa

8

This big brown monster is
harmless to humans.
But it's the heaviest insect
in the world.
It's about the size of your hand
and weighs more than a sparrow.

*It protects itself by using
its own body as a trap.*

SNAP!

*It pinches a monkey's fingers
in the space between its body
and its hard wing covers.*

GIANT BIRD-EATING SPIDER
(Theraphosa leblondi)
Surinam

MEET THE MONSTER SPIDER:
the largest in the world!
Its body is nearly 4 inches long.
Its leg span is up to 11 inches wide!
It weighs almost as much as
a quarter-pounder from McDonald's!

10

When it gets scared, this
giant makes a purring noise.
It rises up on its fourth pair
of legs to look even larger!
Its bite hurts, but isn't
poisonous to humans.

This giant eats insects, small lizards,
and small snakes (even poisonous ones).
It also catches and eats small birds!

*In 1705, Maria Merian published a book
of paintings she did in the Amazon jungle.
One shows a huge spider dragging
a hummingbird from its nest.
Nobody believed her for **158 years**...
**when another scientist finally saw
these spiders killing small birds.***

This giant stabs its prey
with poison fangs up to one inch long.
Its venom turns the inside
of its victim's body to liquid.
Then it sips up the insides.

What do **you** think:
M-M-M-MONSTER?
Or just eating to live?

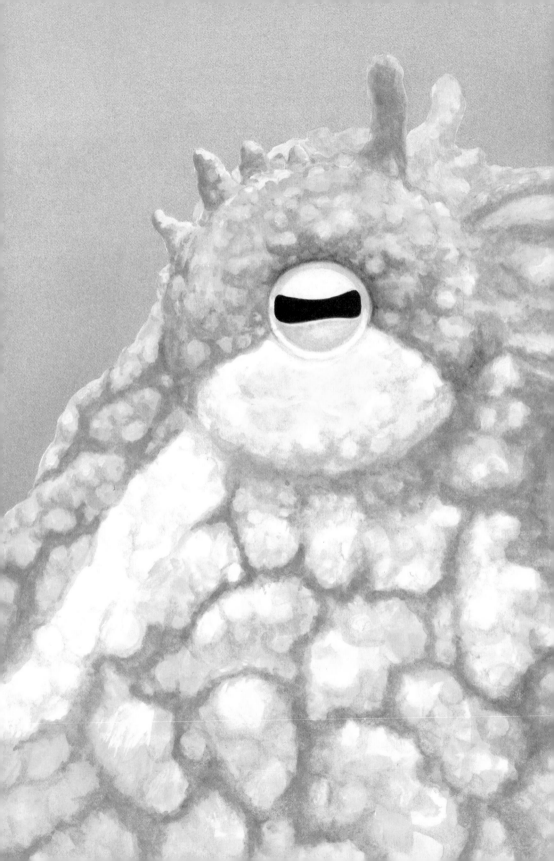

CHAPTER TWO:
GIGANTIC SEA MONSTERS!

GIANT OCTOPUS
(Octopus dolfleini)
Northern Pacific Ocean

This giant eye belongs to a
30-foot monster that lives in the sea—
a monster bigger than
a merry-go-round.

In the blink of *your* eye,
this monster can turn from
brown to red to maroon to cream . . .
or any shade in between.
It has blue blood.

This monster can squeeze into
a space smaller than its beak . . .
hug you tight . . .
and tiptoe on its arms.

CAN YOU GUESS WHAT IT IS?

It's a giant octopus!

Can you spot a giant octopus
in this picture?
Can you find more than one?
It's not easy.

*How many giant octopuses
can you spot on these pages?*

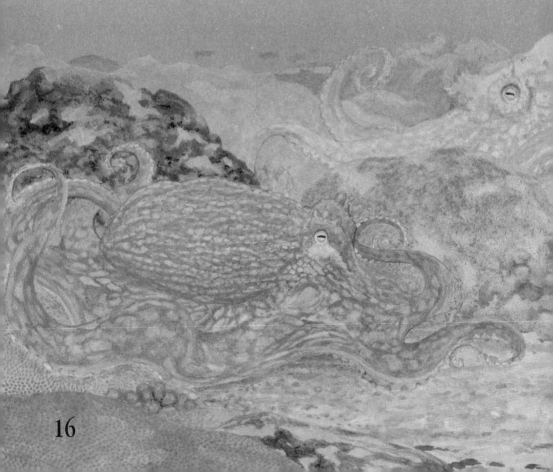

Giant octopuses often hide near
rocks or caves under the sea.
They turn the same colors as the rocks.
Their skin even gets rough to match
the rocks or seaweed nearby.

Their color even gets **darker** when
a shadow passes over them.

Q: How do two octopuses walk along the ocean floor?

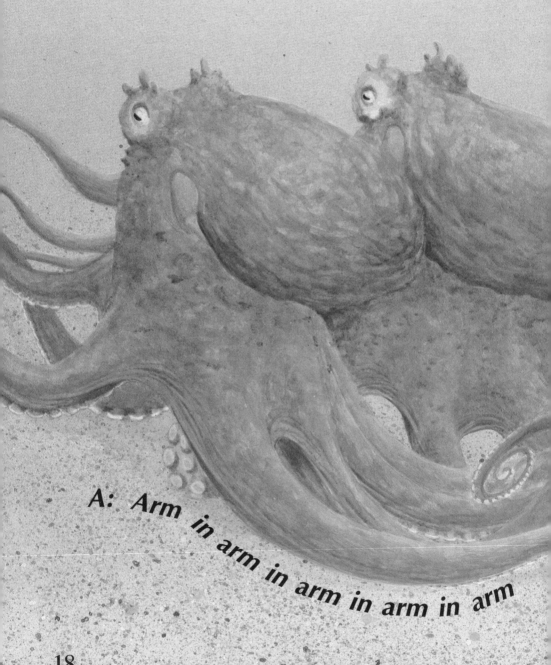

A: Arm in arm in arm in arm in arm in arm

HOW DOES AN OCTOPUS PROTECT ITSELF?

It changes color to hide from enemies.
Its eight strong arms can fight.
Strong suckers help it hold on tight.
And if a very big fish grabs
an octopus by one arm,
the arm can just break off!
Then the octopus swims safely away
and grows a new arm
in just a few months.

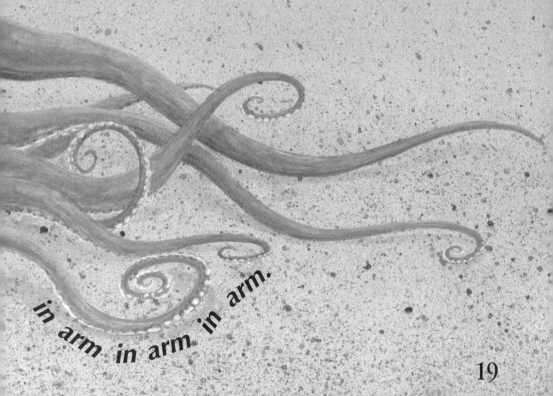

in arm in arm in arm.

An octopus also protects itself by
squirting out dark clouds of ink
shaped just like . . . **AN OCTOPUS!**
The ink even **SMELLS** like an octopus!
While its enemy chases a cloud of ink,
the real octopus can swim safely away.

What's called a fish
but looks like a giant umbrella?
*The **ARCTIC LION'S MANE**—*
the largest jellyfish in the world.

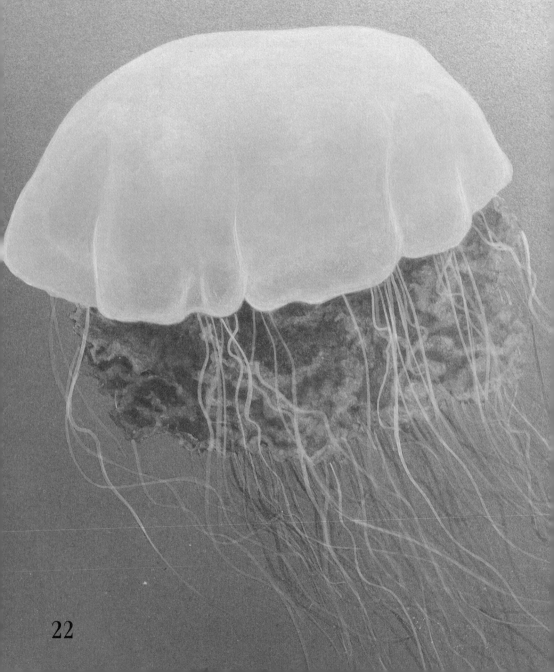

GIANT JELLYFISH or
ARCTIC LION'S MANE
(Cyanea capillata arctica)
Northwestern Atlantic Ocean

Jellyfish aren't really fish.
They're boneless, brainless animals.
They look and feel like Jell-O
because they're almost all water.

Some jellyfish are **as small as grapes**.
But the **Arctic Lion's Mane** is almost
as big as a basketball court.
Its tentacles are 130 feet long!

Jellyfish may look pretty,
but they're full of poison.
They use it to kill the small
sea animals they eat.
Some jellyfish even kill humans!

A giant jellyfish
has many stinging cells
on each of more
than 1,000 tentacles.

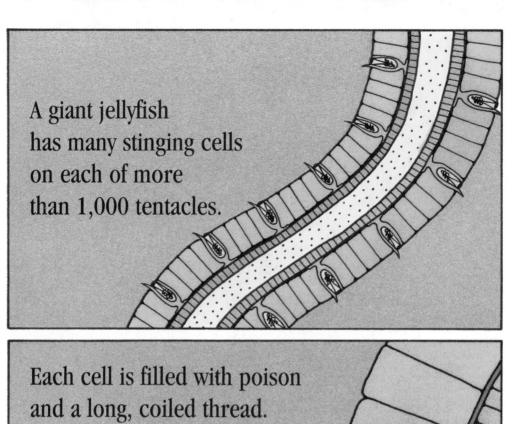

Each cell is filled with poison
and a long, coiled thread.

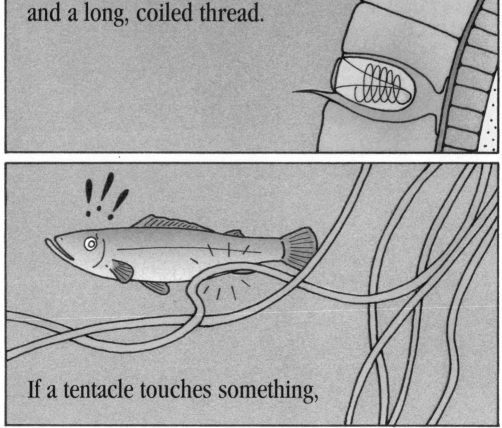

If a tentacle touches something,

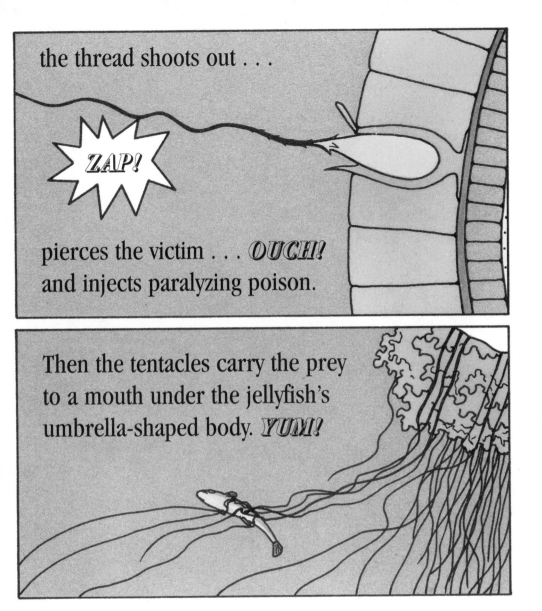

the thread shoots out . . .

ZAP!

pierces the victim . . . *OUCH!* and injects paralyzing poison.

Then the tentacles carry the prey to a mouth under the jellyfish's umbrella-shaped body. *YUM!*

How did the Arctic Lion's Mane get its name?

Hint: *Do its yellow tentacles remind you of another animal?*

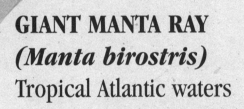

GIANT MANTA RAY
(Manta birostris)
Tropical Atlantic waters

Imagine this giant 23-foot manta ray
spreading its large, dark "wings"
and **FLAPPING** toward you
like a **HUGE UNDERWATER BAT!**

Some call this giant a **DEVILFISH**
because the horns on its head
and the sharp, toothlike points
sticking out of its skin look so **EVIL.**

But don't worry: it won't eat *you!*
Its whiplike tail carries no stinger.
This peaceful giant may be as big
as a school bus, but it spends most
of its time hiding under the sand.
And it never eats people—
just teeny-tiny shrimp
called plankton.

A giant manta ray is 23 feet wide when it
spreads its "wings."
How wide are **you** *when you spread*
your arms?
Measure . . . then compare!

Mantas live in the sea, but some
manta pups are born in midair!
Scientists have seen groups of female
mantas leap out of the sea to give birth.

The pup seems to fly out of its mother.
Then the mother falls back into the sea
with a sound like a giant clap of thunder!

The manta pup is born with its
"wings" neatly folded.
It looks just like its mother.
It has all it needs to survive.
And it's 4 feet long—just about your size!

How tall are you?
Are you TALLER or shorter than
A BABY GIANT MANTA?

CHAPTER THREE:
THE MORE, THE MEANER!

ARMY ANTS:
(Dorylus)
Africa and tropical Asia

What's that dark red flood
spreading across the ground?
Is it blood?

And what's that crackling, hissing sound?
Is it rain pattering through the trees?

No! It's **20 MILLION ARMY ANTS**
on the march in search of food.
That's more than all the people in
New York City!

They flow like a slow-moving river
across the forest floor.
Moving about 60 feet an hour,
army ants work together
to circle and trap an enemy.
Then they attack from all sides.

This is a life-size army ant.
Would you say it looks small? Harmless?
GUESS AGAIN! *For its size, this is*
the most powerful insect in the world.

One bite can snip off a grasshopper's leg
...or cut a tiny gash in a snake or a person.
Army ants eat only live, *fresh* food
that they catch and kill!

A swarm can tear whole cows to pieces
within minutes.
Army ants even attack humans.

A hungry swarm of army ants
will eat anything alive in its path.
So when the ants go marching
one million by one million,
**YOU BETTER GET OUT
OF THEIR WAY!**

PIRANHAS
(Serrasalmus nattereri)
South America

These savage killers move in mobs
of a hundred or a thousand,
searching for their next meal.
When they smell or taste blood,
they go into a feeding frenzy.

They attack large living animals
like horses, cows, or humans.
In minutes, they strip away
every shred of flesh . . .
leaving nothing but bones.

South American piranhas
in a feeding frenzy

A piranha has powerful jaws.
Its **RAZOR-SHARP TEETH**
snap sharply together.

A piranha can chop off your toe
or finger as quickly as an ax.
It can bite through fishhooks
or chunks of wood.
It may be
**THE MOST
DANGEROUS
FISH
IN THE
WORLD!**

*And believe it or not,
each piranha is only
about one foot long!*

LEECHES
(many species)
all over the world

Leeches are worms that live by
sucking blood from their victims.
A leech uses its suckers
to **CLING** to its prey.
Then its sharp mouth parts
SAW into the skin.

A special liquid keeps the
blood from clotting.
It also numbs the wound so the
victim can't feel the leech suck.

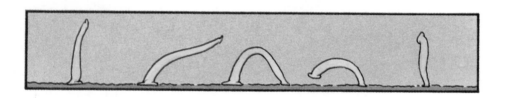

Leeches move by crawling, flipping,
or swimming.
They use their suckers to pull
themselves along.

Only some leeches are dangerous.
Others can help cure illness.
For thousands of years,
leeches were used to suck poison
out of snake and insect bites.

Today scientists study leeches to find
ways to prevent heart attacks.
If they can find what leeches use to
keep blood from clotting, it might
help prevent heart attacks in humans.

All these leeches are life-size!

39

CHAPTER FOUR:
REAL LIVE DRAGONS!

KOMODO DRAGONS
(Varanus komodoensis)
Indonesia

What living monster has three eyes,
smells like a rotten garbage pail,
eats animals the size of a small bus,
and SOMETIMES HUNTS HUMANS?

The Komodo dragon!
The world's largest living lizard.

Yes, Komodo dragons are **real!**
But don't look over your shoulder.
The world's largest lizards live only
on six small islands near Indonesia.

Lucky! You may not want
to meet one in a dark alley.
A Komodo dragon has a forked tongue;
long, sharp claws;
and **RAZOR-SHARP TEETH**.
Its tail slashes from side to side
like a sharp sword.
Its body is covered with rough scales
like a suit of armor.

The largest Komodo ever measured was
10 feet long and weighed 365 pounds.
Most Komodos are 5 to 9 feet long.
Since they can swallow animals
about as big as they are, their weight
depends on how recently they ate . . .
and how huge the meal was!

*What do you think this guy weighs
after he eats lunch?*

10'2.5" Komodo weighs 365 lbs.

Komodo dragons kill water buffalo
that weigh as much as 1300 pounds.
They tear them up
and eat the insides first.

They eat mice, monkeys, deer,
wild boar, and poisonous snakes.
They even settle for **DEAD** animals,
like **ROTTEN** fish or crabs.
(Now do you know why they stink?)

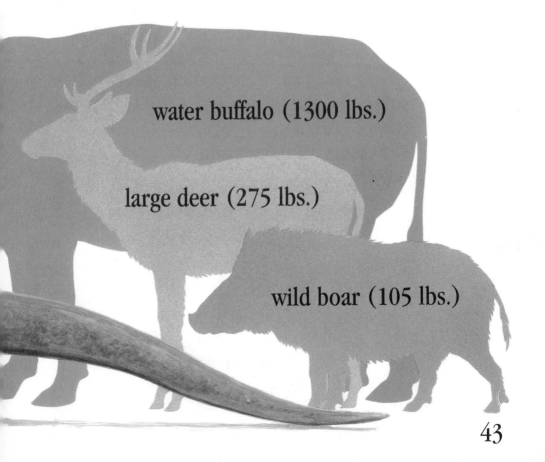

water buffalo (1300 lbs.)

large deer (275 lbs.)

wild boar (105 lbs.)

Imagine a Komodo hunting.
It hides in tall grass, waiting to jump.
It's the same drab gray as the dirt.
It rears up on its strong back legs,
using its tail for balance.

Then it **LUNGES**,
grabbing the victim in its mouth.
It swallows it whole!

Komodo dragons are meat-eaters.
They don't usually dine on humans.
They may look toothless, but **BEWARE!**
Sixty huge, sharp teeth are hiding
under those spongy pink gums.
And they have plenty of spares!

Komodo dragons get up to
200 new teeth a year
to replace old or lost ones.
(We humans get only 52 in our whole life!)

*Compare your teeth
to one of these!
It's a life-size tooth
from a Komodo dragon.*

A Komodo is a **THREE-EYED MONSTER!**
It has two sharp eyes in front.
Can you find its third eye?
It's under a small, clear scale
like a window on top of its head.

Try facing a bright light with your eyes closed.
That's about what a Komodo dragon's
third eye sees.

Q: How do you think this helps the Komodo?
A: It helps sense when enemies are near.

46

Komodo dragons have been around
for at least *20 million years.*
They can survive hot dry spells
up to 130 degrees Fahrenheit,
flooding rains,
even the earthquakes and volcanoes
that often shake their islands.
The big question now is:
***Can they survive the ways humans
are hurting their island homes?***

YOU HAVE THE LAST WORD ON
MONSTERS!

Now that you've met the monsters,
WHAT DO YOU THINK?

Scientists don't call animals
"good" or "bad."
Instead, they watch how animals
hunt, eat, and protect themselves.
Scientists also try to find out
what animals must do to stay alive.

**Look again at the "monsters"
in this book.**
Try to see them the way scientists do.
Then decide for yourself:
are they **AWFUL** . . .
or **AWESOME?**